Monthly Pla

MW00917158

Month: ________ **Year:** ________

Monday	Tuesday	Wednesday	Thursday	Friday	Saturday	Sunday

Notes:

Monthly Planner

Month: ________ **Year:** ________

Monday	Tuesday	Wednesday	Thursday	Friday	Saturday	Sunday

Notes:

Monthly Planner

Month: ________ Year: ________

Monday	Tuesday	Wednesday	Thursday	Friday	Saturday	Sunday

Notes:

Monthly Planner

Month: ________ **Year:** ________

Monday	Tuesday	Wednesday	Thursday	Friday	Saturday	Sunday

Notes:

Monthly Planner

Month: ________ **Year:** ________

Monday	Tuesday	Wednesday	Thursday	Friday	Saturday	Sunday

Notes:

Monthly Planner

Month: ________ **Year:** ________

Monday	Tuesday	Wednesday	Thursday	Friday	Saturday	Sunday

Notes:

Monthly Planner

Month: ________ **Year:** ________

Monday	Tuesday	Wednesday	Thursday	Friday	Saturday	Sunday

Notes:

Monthly Planner

Month: ________ **Year:** ________

Monday	Tuesday	Wednesday	Thursday	Friday	Saturday	Sunday

Notes:

Monthly Planner

Month: ________ **Year:** ________

Monday	Tuesday	Wednesday	Thursday	Friday	Saturday	Sunday

Notes:

Monthly Planner

Month: ________ **Year:** ________

Monday	Tuesday	Wednesday	Thursday	Friday	Saturday	Sunday

Notes:

Monthly Planner

Month: ________ **Year:** ________

Monday	Tuesday	Wednesday	Thursday	Friday	Saturday	Sunday

Notes:

Monthly Planner

Month: ________ **Year:** ________

Monday	Tuesday	Wednesday	Thursday	Friday	Saturday	Sunday

Notes:

Monthly Planner

Month: ________ **Year:** ________

Monday	Tuesday	Wednesday	Thursday	Friday	Saturday	Sunday

Notes:

Monthly Planner

Month: ________ **Year:** ________

Monday	Tuesday	Wednesday	Thursday	Friday	Saturday	Sunday

Notes:

Monthly Planner

Month: ________ **Year:** ________

Monday	Tuesday	Wednesday	Thursday	Friday	Saturday	Sunday
☐	☐	☐	☐	☐	☐	☐
☐	☐	☐	☐	☐	☐	☐
☐	☐	☐	☐	☐	☐	☐
☐	☐	☐	☐	☐	☐	☐
☐	☐	☐	☐	☐	☐	☐

Notes:

Monthly Planner

Month: ________ **Year:** ________

Monday	Tuesday	Wednesday	Thursday	Friday	Saturday	Sunday

Notes:

Monthly Planner

Month: ________ **Year:** ________

Monday	Tuesday	Wednesday	Thursday	Friday	Saturday	Sunday

Notes:

Monthly Planner

Month: ________ **Year:** ________

Monday	Tuesday	Wednesday	Thursday	Friday	Saturday	Sunday

Notes:

Monthly Planner

Month: ________ **Year:** ________

Monday	Tuesday	Wednesday	Thursday	Friday	Saturday	Sunday

Notes:

Monthly Planner

Month: ________ **Year:** ________

Monday	Tuesday	Wednesday	Thursday	Friday	Saturday	Sunday

Notes:

Monthly Planner

Month: ________ **Year:** ________

Monday	Tuesday	Wednesday	Thursday	Friday	Saturday	Sunday

Notes:

Monthly Planner

Month: ________ **Year:** ________

Monday	Tuesday	Wednesday	Thursday	Friday	Saturday	Sunday

Notes:

Monthly Planner

Month: ________ **Year:** ________

Monday	Tuesday	Wednesday	Thursday	Friday	Saturday	Sunday

Notes:

Monthly Planner

Month: ________ **Year:** ________

Monday	Tuesday	Wednesday	Thursday	Friday	Saturday	Sunday

Notes:

Monthly Planner

Month: ________ **Year:** ________

Monday	Tuesday	Wednesday	Thursday	Friday	Saturday	Sunday

Notes:

Monthly Planner

Month: ________ **Year:** ________

Monday	Tuesday	Wednesday	Thursday	Friday	Saturday	Sunday

Notes:

Monthly Planner

Month: ________ **Year:** ________

Monday	Tuesday	Wednesday	Thursday	Friday	Saturday	Sunday

Notes:

Monthly Planner

Month: ________ **Year:** ________

Monday	Tuesday	Wednesday	Thursday	Friday	Saturday	Sunday

Notes:

Monthly Planner

Month: ________ **Year:** ________

Monday	Tuesday	Wednesday	Thursday	Friday	Saturday	Sunday

Notes:

Monthly Planner

Month: ________ **Year:** ________

Monday	Tuesday	Wednesday	Thursday	Friday	Saturday	Sunday

Notes:

Monthly Planner

Month: ________ **Year:** ________

Monday	Tuesday	Wednesday	Thursday	Friday	Saturday	Sunday

Notes:

Monthly Planner

Month: ________ **Year:** ________

Monday	Tuesday	Wednesday	Thursday	Friday	Saturday	Sunday

Notes:

Monthly Planner

Month: ________ **Year:** ________

Monday	Tuesday	Wednesday	Thursday	Friday	Saturday	Sunday

Notes:

Monthly Planner

Month: ______ **Year:** ______

Monday	Tuesday	Wednesday	Thursday	Friday	Saturday	Sunday

Notes:

Monthly Planner

Month: ________ **Year:** ________

Monday	Tuesday	Wednesday	Thursday	Friday	Saturday	Sunday

Notes:

Monthly Planner

Month: ________ **Year:** ________

Monday	Tuesday	Wednesday	Thursday	Friday	Saturday	Sunday

Notes:

Monthly Planner

Month: ______ **Year:** ______

Monday	Tuesday	Wednesday	Thursday	Friday	Saturday	Sunday

Notes:

Monthly Planner

Month: ________ **Year:** ________

Monday	Tuesday	Wednesday	Thursday	Friday	Saturday	Sunday

Notes:

Monthly Planner

Month: ________ **Year:** ________

Monday	Tuesday	Wednesday	Thursday	Friday	Saturday	Sunday
☐	☐	☐	☐	☐	☐	☐
☐	☐	☐	☐	☐	☐	☐
☐	☐	☐	☐	☐	☐	☐
☐	☐	☐	☐	☐	☐	☐
☐	☐	☐	☐	☐	☐	☐

Notes:

Monthly Planner

Month: ________ **Year:** ________

Monday	Tuesday	Wednesday	Thursday	Friday	Saturday	Sunday

Notes:

Monthly Planner

Month: ________ **Year:** ________

Monday	Tuesday	Wednesday	Thursday	Friday	Saturday	Sunday

Notes:

Monthly Planner

Month: ________ **Year:** ________

Monday	Tuesday	Wednesday	Thursday	Friday	Saturday	Sunday

Notes:

Monthly Planner

Month: ________ **Year:** ________

Monday	Tuesday	Wednesday	Thursday	Friday	Saturday	Sunday

Notes:

Monthly Planner

Month: ________ **Year:** ________

Monday	Tuesday	Wednesday	Thursday	Friday	Saturday	Sunday

Notes:

Monthly Planner

Month: ________ **Year:** ________

Monday	Tuesday	Wednesday	Thursday	Friday	Saturday	Sunday

Notes:

Monthly Planner

Month: ________ **Year:** ________

Monday	Tuesday	Wednesday	Thursday	Friday	Saturday	Sunday

Notes:

Monthly Planner

Month: ________ **Year:** ________

Monday	Tuesday	Wednesday	Thursday	Friday	Saturday	Sunday

Notes:

Monthly Planner

Month: ________ **Year:** ________

Monday	Tuesday	Wednesday	Thursday	Friday	Saturday	Sunday

Notes:

Monthly Planner

Month: ________ **Year:** ________

Monday	Tuesday	Wednesday	Thursday	Friday	Saturday	Sunday

Notes:

Monthly Planner

Month: ________ **Year:** ________

Monday	Tuesday	Wednesday	Thursday	Friday	Saturday	Sunday

Notes:

Monthly Planner

Month: ________ **Year:** ________

Monday	Tuesday	Wednesday	Thursday	Friday	Saturday	Sunday

Notes:

Monthly Planner

Month: ________ **Year:** ________

Monday	Tuesday	Wednesday	Thursday	Friday	Saturday	Sunday

Notes:

Monthly Planner

Month: ________ **Year:** ________

Monday	Tuesday	Wednesday	Thursday	Friday	Saturday	Sunday

Notes:

Monthly Planner

Month: ________ **Year:** ________

Monday	Tuesday	Wednesday	Thursday	Friday	Saturday	Sunday

Notes:

Monthly Planner

Month: ________ **Year:** ________

Monday	Tuesday	Wednesday	Thursday	Friday	Saturday	Sunday

Notes:

Monthly Planner

Month: ________ **Year:** ________

Monday	Tuesday	Wednesday	Thursday	Friday	Saturday	Sunday

Notes:

Monthly Planner

Month: ________ **Year:** ________

Monday	Tuesday	Wednesday	Thursday	Friday	Saturday	Sunday

Notes:

Monthly Planner

Month: ________ **Year:** ________

Monday	Tuesday	Wednesday	Thursday	Friday	Saturday	Sunday

Notes:

Monthly Planner

Month: ________ **Year:** ________

Monday	Tuesday	Wednesday	Thursday	Friday	Saturday	Sunday

Notes:

Monthly Planner

Month: ________ **Year:** ________

Monday	Tuesday	Wednesday	Thursday	Friday	Saturday	Sunday

Notes:

Monthly Planner

Month: ________ **Year:** ________

Monday	Tuesday	Wednesday	Thursday	Friday	Saturday	Sunday
☐	☐	☐	☐	☐	☐	☐
☐	☐	☐	☐	☐	☐	☐
☐	☐	☐	☐	☐	☐	☐
☐	☐	☐	☐	☐	☐	☐
☐	☐	☐	☐	☐	☐	☐

Notes:

Monthly Planner

Month: ________ **Year:** ________

Monday	Tuesday	Wednesday	Thursday	Friday	Saturday	Sunday

Notes:

Monthly Planner

Month: ________ **Year:** ________

Monday	Tuesday	Wednesday	Thursday	Friday	Saturday	Sunday

Notes:

Monthly Planner

Month: ________ **Year:** ________

Monday	Tuesday	Wednesday	Thursday	Friday	Saturday	Sunday

Notes:

Monthly Planner

Month: ________ **Year:** ________

Monday	Tuesday	Wednesday	Thursday	Friday	Saturday	Sunday

Notes:

Monthly Planner

Month: ________ **Year:** ________

Monday	Tuesday	Wednesday	Thursday	Friday	Saturday	Sunday

Notes:

Monthly Planner

Month: ________ **Year:** ________

Monday	Tuesday	Wednesday	Thursday	Friday	Saturday	Sunday

Notes:

Monthly Planner

Month: ________ **Year:** ________

Monday	Tuesday	Wednesday	Thursday	Friday	Saturday	Sunday

Notes:

Monthly Planner

Month: ________ **Year:** ________

Monday	Tuesday	Wednesday	Thursday	Friday	Saturday	Sunday

Notes:

Monthly Planner

Month: ________ **Year:** ________

Monday	Tuesday	Wednesday	Thursday	Friday	Saturday	Sunday

Notes:

Monthly Planner

Month: ________ **Year:** ________

Monday	Tuesday	Wednesday	Thursday	Friday	Saturday	Sunday

Notes:

Monthly Planner

Month: ________ **Year:** ________

Monday	Tuesday	Wednesday	Thursday	Friday	Saturday	Sunday

Notes:

Monthly Planner

Month: ________ **Year:** ________

Monday	Tuesday	Wednesday	Thursday	Friday	Saturday	Sunday

Notes:

Monthly Planner

Month: ________ Year: ________

Monday	Tuesday	Wednesday	Thursday	Friday	Saturday	Sunday
☐	☐	☐	☐	☐	☐	☐
☐	☐	☐	☐	☐	☐	☐
☐	☐	☐	☐	☐	☐	☐
☐	☐	☐	☐	☐	☐	☐
☐	☐	☐	☐	☐	☐	☐

Notes:

Monthly Planner

Month: ________ **Year:** ________

Monday	Tuesday	Wednesday	Thursday	Friday	Saturday	Sunday

Notes:

Monthly Planner

Month: ________ **Year:** ________

Monday	Tuesday	Wednesday	Thursday	Friday	Saturday	Sunday

Notes:

Monthly Planner

Month: ________ **Year:** ________

Monday	Tuesday	Wednesday	Thursday	Friday	Saturday	Sunday

Notes:

Monthly Planner

Month: ________ Year: ________

Monday	Tuesday	Wednesday	Thursday	Friday	Saturday	Sunday
☐	☐	☐	☐	☐	☐	☐
☐	☐	☐	☐	☐	☐	☐
☐	☐	☐	☐	☐	☐	☐
☐	☐	☐	☐	☐	☐	☐
☐	☐	☐	☐	☐	☐	☐

Notes:

Monthly Planner

Month: ________ **Year:** ________

Monday	Tuesday	Wednesday	Thursday	Friday	Saturday	Sunday

Notes:

Monthly Planner

Month: ________ Year: ________

Monday	Tuesday	Wednesday	Thursday	Friday	Saturday	Sunday

Notes:

Monthly Planner

Month: ________ **Year:** ________

Monday	Tuesday	Wednesday	Thursday	Friday	Saturday	Sunday

Notes:

Monthly Planner

Month: ________ **Year:** ________

Monday	Tuesday	Wednesday	Thursday	Friday	Saturday	Sunday

Notes:

Monthly Planner

Month: ________ Year: ________

Monday	Tuesday	Wednesday	Thursday	Friday	Saturday	Sunday

Notes:

Monthly Planner

Month: ________ Year: ________

Monday	Tuesday	Wednesday	Thursday	Friday	Saturday	Sunday
☐	☐	☐	☐	☐	☐	☐
☐	☐	☐	☐	☐	☐	☐
☐	☐	☐	☐	☐	☐	☐
☐	☐	☐	☐	☐	☐	☐
☐	☐	☐	☐	☐	☐	☐

Notes:

Monthly Planner

Month: ________ **Year:** ________

Monday	Tuesday	Wednesday	Thursday	Friday	Saturday	Sunday

Notes:

Monthly Planner

Month: ________ **Year:** ________

Monday	Tuesday	Wednesday	Thursday	Friday	Saturday	Sunday

Notes:

Monthly Planner

Month: ________ **Year:** ________

Monday	Tuesday	Wednesday	Thursday	Friday	Saturday	Sunday
☐	☐	☐	☐	☐	☐	☐
☐	☐	☐	☐	☐	☐	☐
☐	☐	☐	☐	☐	☐	☐
☐	☐	☐	☐	☐	☐	☐
☐	☐	☐	☐	☐	☐	☐

Notes:

Monthly Planner

Month: ________ **Year:** ________

Monday	Tuesday	Wednesday	Thursday	Friday	Saturday	Sunday

Notes:

Monthly Planner

Month: ________ **Year:** ________

Monday	Tuesday	Wednesday	Thursday	Friday	Saturday	Sunday

Notes:

Monthly Planner

Month: ________ **Year:** ________

Monday	Tuesday	Wednesday	Thursday	Friday	Saturday	Sunday

Notes:

Monthly Planner

Month: ________ **Year:** ________

Monday	Tuesday	Wednesday	Thursday	Friday	Saturday	Sunday

Notes:

Monthly Planner

Month: ________ **Year:** ________

Monday	Tuesday	Wednesday	Thursday	Friday	Saturday	Sunday

Notes:

Monthly Planner

Month: ________ **Year:** ________

Monday	Tuesday	Wednesday	Thursday	Friday	Saturday	Sunday

Notes:

Monthly Planner

Month: ________ **Year:** ________

Monday	Tuesday	Wednesday	Thursday	Friday	Saturday	Sunday

Notes:

Monthly Planner

Month: ________ Year: ________

Monday	Tuesday	Wednesday	Thursday	Friday	Saturday	Sunday

Notes:

Monthly Planner

Month: _______ Year: _______

Monday	Tuesday	Wednesday	Thursday	Friday	Saturday	Sunday
☐	☐	☐	☐	☐	☐	☐
☐	☐	☐	☐	☐	☐	☐
☐	☐	☐	☐	☐	☐	☐
☐	☐	☐	☐	☐	☐	☐
☐	☐	☐	☐	☐	☐	☐

Notes:

Monthly Planner

Month: ________ **Year:** ________

Monday	Tuesday	Wednesday	Thursday	Friday	Saturday	Sunday

Notes:

Monthly Planner

Month: ______ **Year:** ______

Monday	Tuesday	Wednesday	Thursday	Friday	Saturday	Sunday

Notes:

Monthly Planner

Month: ________ **Year:** ________

Monday	Tuesday	Wednesday	Thursday	Friday	Saturday	Sunday

Notes:

Monthly Planner

Month: ________ **Year:** ________

Monday	Tuesday	Wednesday	Thursday	Friday	Saturday	Sunday

Notes:

Monthly Planner

Month: ________ **Year:** ________

Monday	Tuesday	Wednesday	Thursday	Friday	Saturday	Sunday

Notes:

Monthly Planner

Month: ________ **Year:** ________

Monday	Tuesday	Wednesday	Thursday	Friday	Saturday	Sunday

Notes:

Monthly Planner

Month: ________ Year: ________

Monday	Tuesday	Wednesday	Thursday	Friday	Saturday	Sunday

Notes:

Monthly Planner

Month: ________ **Year:** ________

Monday	Tuesday	Wednesday	Thursday	Friday	Saturday	Sunday

Notes:

Monthly Planner

Month: ________ **Year:** ________

Monday	Tuesday	Wednesday	Thursday	Friday	Saturday	Sunday

Notes:

Monthly Planner

Month: ________ **Year:** ________

Monday	Tuesday	Wednesday	Thursday	Friday	Saturday	Sunday

Notes:

Monthly Planner

Month: ________ **Year:** ________

Monday	Tuesday	Wednesday	Thursday	Friday	Saturday	Sunday

Notes:

Monthly Planner

Month: ________ Year: ________

Monday	Tuesday	Wednesday	Thursday	Friday	Saturday	Sunday

Notes:

Monthly Planner

Month: ________ **Year:** ________

Monday	Tuesday	Wednesday	Thursday	Friday	Saturday	Sunday

Notes:

Monthly Planner

Month: ________ **Year:** ________

Monday	Tuesday	Wednesday	Thursday	Friday	Saturday	Sunday

Notes:

Made in the USA
Monee, IL
15 July 2022

99783118R00066